TITCHY WITCH

and the

Bully
Boggarts

For Isobel Louise - welcome
R.I.

To Kath
K.M.

Orchard Books
96 Leonard Street, London EC2A 4XD
Orchard Books Australia
32/45-51 Huntley Street, Alexandria, NSW 2015
First published in Great Britain in 2003
First paperback publication 2004
ISBN 1 84121 048 X (HB)
ISBN 1 84121 124 9 (PB)
Text © Rose Impey 2003 Illustrations © Katharine McEwen 2003
The rights of Rose Impey to be identified as the author and
Katharine McEwen to be identified as the illustrator of this Work
have been asserted by them in accordance with the
Copyright, Designs and Patents Act, 1988.
A CIP catalogue record for this book is available from the British Library
1 3 5 7 9 10 8 6 4 2 (HB)
3 5 7 9 10 8 6 4 2 (PB)
Printed in Hong Kong

TITCHY WITCH

and the

Bully Boggarts

Rose Impey ★ Katharine McEwen

ORCHARD BOOKS

Titchy-witch

Victor

Eric

Wendel

Weeny-witch

Witchy-witch

Cat-a-bogus

Titchy-witch didn't want to
go to school. She said she had
a tummy-ache.

"Too many Grobble Gums,"
said Cat-a-bogus.

"All little witches have to go to school," said Mum.

"Even this little witch," said Dad.

Titchy-witch wanted Mum to take her to school, but Witchy-witch was too busy with the baby.

So Cat-a-bogus took her instead
and Titchy-witch scowled all
the way.

She didn't want anyone to see her
being taken to school by a cat!
But Gobby-goblin saw her.

When Titchy-witch stuck her nose in the air, the little goblin tripped her up.

So Titchy-witch turned his nose
into a sausage.

It soon turned back, but it still
made him mad.

Gobby-goblin's brother was a
terrible bully.
He stood on Titchy-witch's foot
and twisted her arm behind
her back.

So she turned his head into
a cabbage.

"You wait," said the cabbage.
"After school, we'll get our cousins
onto you. They're boggarts!"

But Titchy-witch didn't even wait
for Cat-a-bogus.
She set off home on her own.

When Titchy-witch was
half-way home, she heard a
whis-whis-whispering sound.

She knew what it was.
You could smell boggarts a mile
away.

Seven of them jumped out of the bushes. (Boggarts always travel in gangs. They're so stupid they'd get lost on their own.)

Titchy-witch wasn't afraid of one
boggart. But seven!

The boggarts called her names:

And pulled her hair and pinched
her hat.

They tried to make Titchy-witch
cry, but even little witches
never cry.

"My dad will turn you all into toads," she said bravely.
"Let him," croaked the boggarts.

"My mum will turn you all into pigs," she said.

"Who cares," grunted the boggarts.

Then Titchy-witch had
a great idea.
She made up a spell:

"Pinch of sugar, pinch of spice.
All things pink and sweet and nice.
Turn these boggarts, brown and hairy,
Into little boggart-fairies."

The boggarts stared at each other
and started to squeal.

When they saw Cat-a-bogus coming, the fairy-boggarts ran away.

Cat-a-bogus told Titchy-witch she was getting too big for her broomstick.

He made her promise she would always wait for him from now on.

Cat-a-bogus was glad she'd learned her lesson, for once.

But Titchy-witch was planning
a little lesson of her own.

TITCHY WITCH

Rose Impey ★ Katharine McEwen

Enjoy a little more magic with all the Titchy-witch tales:

- ❏ Titchy-witch and the Birthday Broomstick   1 84121 120 6
- ❏ Titchy-witch and the Disappearing Baby   1 84121 116 8
- ❏ Titchy-witch and the Frog Fiasco   1 84121 122 2
- ❏ Titchy-witch and the Stray Dragon   1 8. 118 4
- ❏ Titchy-witch and the Bully-Boggarts   1 8412. 9
- ❏ Titch -witch and the Wobbly Fang   1 84121 126 5
- ❏ Ti _ ɔ-witch and the Get-Better Spell   1 84121 128 1
- ❏ T.tchy-witch and the Magic Party   1 84121 130 3

All priced at £4.99 each

Colour Crunchies are available from all good
bookshops, or can be ordered direct from the publisher:
Orchard Books, PO BOX 29, Douglas IM99 1BQ
Credit card orders please telephone 01624 836000
or fax 01624 837033
or e-mail: bookshop@enterprise.net for details.

To order please quote title, author and ISBN
and your full name and address.
Cheques and postal orders should be
made payable to 'Bookpost plc'.
Postage and packing is FREE within the UK
(overseas customers should add £1.00 per book).

Prices and availability are subject to change.